D0458835

BRAINS
FOR LUNCH

BRAINS FOR LUNCH:

A ZOMBIE NOVEL IN HAIKU?!

K. A. HOLT

DRAWINGS BY Gahan Wilson

A NEAL PORTER BOOK
ROARING BROOK PRESS
NEW YORK

Text copyright © 2010 by Kari Anne Roy

Illustrations copyright © 2010 by Gahan Wilson

A Neal Porter Book

Published by Roaring Brook Press

Roaring Brook Press is a division of Holtzbrinck Publishing Holdings

Limited Partnership

175 Fifth Avenue, New York, New York 10010

www.roaringbrookpress.com

Distributed in Canada by H. B. Fenn and Company Ltd.

Library of Congress Cataloging-in-Publication Data

Holt, K. A.

Brains for lunch : a zombie novel in haiku?! / K.A. Holt ; illustrated by Gahan
Wilson.

p. cm.

"A Neal Porter book."

Summary: At a middle school where zombies, blood-sucking chupacabras,
and humans never mingle, "lifer" Siobhan and Loeb, a zombie who likes to
write haiku, share an attraction. Story written entirely in haiku.

ISBN 978-1-59643-629-9

[1. Novels in verse. 2. Zombies—Fiction. 3. Prejudices—Fiction. 4. Middle
schools—Fiction. 5. Schools—Fiction.] I. Wilson, Gahan, ill. II. Title.

PZ7.5.H65Br 2010

[Fic]—dc22

2010012958

Roaring Brook Press books are available for special promotions and premiums.
For details contact: Director of Special Markets, Holtzbrinck Publishers.

First Edition August 2010

Book design by Jennifer Browne

Printed in July 2010 in the United States of America

by RR Donnelley & Sons Company, Crawfordsville, Indiana

1   3   5   7   9   10   8   6   4   2

For Sam, Georgia, and Ike.
If you guys were zombies I'd totally let you eat my brain.
And for Ogden Nash, whose poetry made
my middle school zombie days a lot less boring.

—K. R.

Lunch

Brains for lunch again
"Stop moaning and just eat it."
Lunch lady humor

Dead-on lunchroom stare
Her eyes bore holes like earthworms
Soft and unyielding

"What do you want, Mags?"
I mouth words over the din
"You want my pudding?"

An eye roll response
George catches it, hands it back
An eyeball shortstop

Geek table awaits
Larry brags about fresh flesh
He is full of lies

Also full of flies
Charlie Brown's undead Pig Pen
Larry is so gross

Nothing stops my mouth
"Just shut up for once, Larry."
The fly buffet stands

3

"Up yours, Loeb," he says.
Then he gives me the finger
I give it back. Yuck.

"Leave Loeb alone, yo.
And move your stinking carcass."
That's Matt. He's my friend.

Larry staggers off
"Stupid, fat, fly-filled dodo."
Matt feels brave, I guess

Dissonant buzzing
Larry returns for round two
Matt gives me his tray

I step between them
Could lunch be any more dumb?
Larry takes a swing

My jawbone takes flight
I'm always in the middle
"Break it up, you guys!"

It's Mrs. Fincher
Why's the librarian here?
I guess she eats, too

"Go get your jaw, Loeb."
If my jaw was still attached
It would fall open

How does she know me?
I only gaze from afar
"Loeb! Go. Get. Your. Jaw."

It is on Mags tray
Of course that's where it would land
"Just can't shut your mouth."

Maggie grins at me
Her eyes, though, are not smiling
She hands me my bone

"Sorry 'bout that, Mags."
There's a satisfying pop
She just stares at me

Chairs are scattering
Seven minutes 'til late bell
Brain pudding, wasted

Matt's at my locker
"Makes you smarter, my main man."
He leans over me

Give him dirty look
"What are you talking about?"
"Smell my neck, playa."

"Sweat from a Lifer."
A bottle shakes in my face
Drops cling to its side

"Where did you get that?"
Matt cocks his head to the left
"From the Lifer quad?!"

I'm incredulous
"Crossed the invisible line?
You're that desperate?"

"That line is stupid."
Matt shakes the bottle again
"De-seg says it is."

Hair clumps in place. Check.
"And look how well de-seg works."
I gestured around

Only Zs right here
Not a Lifer to be seen
They keep their distance

"There's a girl. Siobhan."
I eyed him skeptically
"I think she likes me."

Matt and a Lifer?
"Did she sell you that bottle?"
Poor, gullible Matt

The tardy bell rings
Stupid bell. And stupid Matt.
"She doesn't like you!"

"Well, I don't like YOU!"
Matt yelling. A big surprise.
Lifer sweat. I laugh.

Down, down, down the hall
Make it to classroom. Door locked.
Too many tardies

I see Mags in there
Window hatching looks like tats
Mags the Maori

She sees me out here
Her lipless smile, endearing
No wait. It's mocking.

Mags is stupid, too
I point at the lock. Some help?
Mags just waves good-bye

Thanks a lot, Maggie.
Not sure why I whisper it
Need a place to go

Walk past Lifer quad
Someone else is late like me
Her hair, not in clumps

Blackest hair I've seen
Curls around her ears. Ivy.
Her eyes are black, too

I'm . . . inadequate
Hair clumps disheveled so soon
Jawbone on crooked

She smiles from afar
Pushing back her ivy hair
And then, she's running

Lifers. Not my type
Well, usually they're not
I just keep walking

Library

This is where I come
Whether I'm locked out or not
It's my favorite

Mrs. Fincher smiles
Her finger is at her lips
But I am silent

Then, she comes to me
This is when my heart would beat
I remember that

She makes my face flush
Or, I'm just putrefying
Either way, I'm red

"How's your face doing?"
She gently inspects my jaw
This is the best day

"Have you been writing?"
I get redder and redder
"You are so good, Loeb."

Her mouth so pretty
Wish I believed what it said
"Here's a book for you."

"Complicated words
don't always make good stories.
Look at these haiku."

Begrudgingly smile
Small book is light in my hands
Maybe I'll read it

Look at her, stammer
"People think we're dumb, you know.
Stupid Zs, no brains."

Knock knock on my head
"Hello, McFly." She's laughing.
Duck away and scowl

"I think you're smart, Loeb.
Smarter than lots of Lifers."
She whispers that part

She leans in closer
Breath breezes through my ear holes
"Enter the contest."

Shock makes me stagger
No Z ever enters that!
Mrs. Fincher's nuts

"Show off those brains, Loeb.
You have a nice collection."
She punches my arm

Five-seven-five, huh?
Zs would write fly-seven-fly
Tuck book in backpack

I stammer something
And then she's back at her desk
A gorgeous cliché

I sit in the back
Old encyclopedias
Smell like my grandma

See around the stacks
Flitting, hyena laughter
It's Carl the Chupo

"Heya, Carl, what's up."
He shrugs and smiles. His fangs gleem.
"Going to the show?"

"Are you asking, Loeb?"
Ha-ha. Carl thinks he's funny.
A Chupo defect

They've livened things up,
the Chupos getting bused in
Lifers hate them, too

Lifers, Zs, Chupos
A furious melting pot
You should see the fights

I pull out my book
Don't get a chance to read it
Vial under nose

"Yours for twenty bucks."
It's the girl from Lifer quad
"A brain substitute."

I point my finger
and push the vial away
My look says it all

"You don't believe me?"
Ivy hair brushes my book
Avoid eye contact

"Here's a free sample."
Vial drops onto my book
Loudest sigh ever

Can she see through me?
Um, yeah. Pretty sure she can.
I don't mean that way

"So do I eat this?
It sure is small for a snack."
I am playing dumb

"No, no, silly Z.
It's gonna make you smarter.
Homemade bottled brains."

The trouble with Ls
They still think of brains as smarts
But brains are for lunch!

Ignore her again
Push away stupid vial
Try to read my book

"I'm not interested."
"That's fine. Embrace your dumbness."
A smirk, new vial

"Want one for love then?
It'll drive the ladies wild."
She is relentless

Carl is done lurking
"I'll take that one, Lifer girl."
He snatches vial

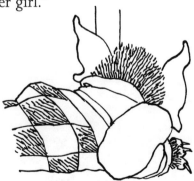

He's off, can't be caught
I laugh, glad she's distracted
Her ivy hair shines

"Be quiet back there."
Mrs. Fincher heard me laugh
Is she a Mrs.?

Library leisure
Surrounded by books and girls
Was that the bell? Dang.

English 101

Weighs as much as George
Collection of past masters
And Omega Man

Speaking of Big George
"'Sup, Loeb." Maggots in his ear
Giving him answers?

"Maggie's new best friend!"
George doesn't get sarcasm
Won't get lost, either

Finally, Matt's here
"All those brains made you late, huh?"
Matt sticks out his tongue

Sweat vial 'round neck
George snatches it away. *Yoink!*
Tosses it to me

Flinch; almost drop it
Vial doesn't smell like sweat.
Toss it back to George

Matt grabs and misses
It's zombie in the middle
He is not laughing

George throws it to him
What a bad throw. Stupid George.
A clatter. A crash.

I'll be a smarty
Lifer sweat on Chuck Taylors
Makes feet a genius

Brief silent moment
Then Matt tries to head-butt George
Use desk as a shield

Teacher starts yelling
A good sound for daydreaming
Look at haiku book

Mags is three rows up
There's a beetle in her hair
Same as yesterday?

She can feel my stare
Briefly turns, glowers at me
Then keeps on reading

Matt's glowering, too
Must beat them both with shovels
When I have the chance

Tonight's the big show
Yearly poetry contest
What if I entered?

Ignore the lesson
Haiku book is really good
Japanese zombies?

A poem tonight
What if I really did it?
In front of whole school!

Wouldn't be so hard
It's how Zs talk anyway
Maybe I should try

Already feel sick
Can't let down Mrs. Fincher
Gonna write haiku

Hallway

Eye poked out again
Bottom lockers really suck
"Hey, Mags! Wait for me!"

"This Zs gotta pee."
"So you ARE talking to me?
Another eye roll

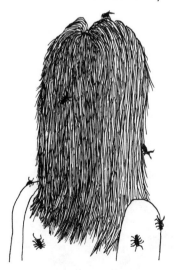 

Catch it, hand it back
"What did I do this time, Mags?"
A withering look

She doesn't scare me
Her wither's worse than her roll.
"She's married, you know."

Mags cuts to the chase
It sure took her long enough
"Who? Mrs. Fincher?"

"Who else, you moron?"
I'm putrefying again
"The way you flirt. Barf."

So incredulous
"You think she thinks that I think—"
"You're such a tool, Loeb."

"And there you have it.
Loeb's idiocy exposed,
His heart is laid bare."

"I'll lay you bare, Matt."
It's my turn to roll my eyes.
Carl. "Stupid Chupo."

"Don't be a racist."
"Don't be a weird goat sucker."
Making it worse, Loeb

"You going tonight?"
Shrug shoulders. Don't want to say.
"Dumb Lifer showcase."

"Think they're all so smart
With their shiny hair and brains.
No way I'm going."

My mouth, opening
Speaking before I can think
"I'm going to go."

All eyes are on me
Maggie is most shocked of all
"Did SHE suggest it?"

"So what if she did?"
Maggie makes kissing noises
Try to ignore her

Carl joins in with her
"Loeb and Fincher in a tree . . .
You like her THAT much?"

Brilliant as ever
"Hey, Carl? Know what you can do?"
The bell drowns me out

No wait. Not the bell
We're a mobile *Thriller* dance
Shuffling out the door

Lifers, Zs, Chupos
All milling around outside
Boy, this should be good

Outside

She is almost close
Ivy-haired girl is right there
She's . . . talking to Matt

I can't help staring
Finger points accusingly
Now they stare at me

Preemptive retort
"Consorting with enemies?"
Big mouth again, Loeb

"Had an accident?"
Her voice is rich, full of life
"Uh," I stammer. "Uh."

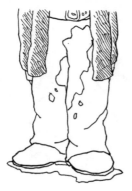

They're laughing at me
Look down and notice something
Guess whose pants are wet?

How did that happen?
Water pistol in Carl's hand
He's one dead Chupo

Take off after him
Carl's no match for zombie speed
I sit on his chest

Matt shambles over
Ivy-haired girl still with him
What is she doing?

"I'll hold down his arms,"
She smiles. "You aim for his brain."
Can she be for real?

Carl is shrieking now
Teachers will be coming soon
Stand up. Met with flies.

"Hey, there. Stupid Loeb."
Larry's just what I need now.
"Step aside, dummy."

"Got a new girlfriend?"
Really don't have time for this
Try to get past him

Walk into flies, fist
Jaw is barely hanging on
"Ut ah ell, arry?"

"That's for lunch today."
"Ooh it *ee* ah unch, arry!"
"Break it up, kiddos."

"Who are you, Lifer?"
Makes a show of sniffing her
"High IQ in there?"

One finger salute
Larry's not a fan of that
This girl is trouble

Carl flits 'round Larry
An unlikely alliance
Crowd is gathering

Mob mentality
As a Z, you know these things
Grab her hand and run

Girl's Lav

In stall together
I feel her breath on my face
Quick puffs, smell like life

Hope there's not a fire
We wait for the all-clear bell
And for mob to pass

Ivy tendrils fall
Dark loops splayed across my arm
Hair, not intestines

Try to play it cool
She's a Lifer after all
I could chomp her brain

"Think the coast is clear?"
I'm finding it hard to talk
"Let's go check it out."

"Wait." I've found my voice.
"What were you doing out there?
You could get eaten."

"It's against the rules."
"What's against the rules? Fighting?"
"No. Eating your peers."

She gives me a smile
"My name is Siobhan," she says.
"That sounds like a car."

Smooth as ever, Loeb.
The stall seems to get smaller
I reach for the latch

She smiles; I stammer
Walk out of stall together
Mags is standing there

"See you later, Loeb."
Can't think of witty response
Mags does it for me

"Bite me, Lifer girl."
Shake head. Mags is so uncouth.
Also, she's unhinged

I try to fix it
Even her nits are seething
She brushes me off

"I can't believe you.
"A teacher AND a Lifer.
You Lothario."

Don't say anything
Smart enough to get away
Just smile; escape fast

But there's no escape
Fincher stands in the doorway
Has Larry by ear

Carl's under her arm
Sack of Chupo potatoes
"You three come with me."

Detention

If scowls could kill you
Mags's face would be a shovel
I'd be dead undead

Desks in the corners
Zs, L, Chupo detention
This one's for you, Hughes

Fincher threatens us
Then she leaves for a meeting
A bad idea

All eyes are on me
They all think this is my fault
Well that just figures

Avoid eye contact
More scared of Mags than Larry
At least I think so

Barely fits in desk
Even Larry's flies are mad
He looks . . . unhappy

Carl is angry, too
He's pointing menacingly
Makes goat sound at me

Siobhan twirls her hair
She is staring at her desk
I see her jaw clench

Only Matt's not mad
Won't stop staring at Siobhan
Whispering "vials"

A microcosm
Whole school boiled down to us
Here in detention

Everyone hates me?
That's not such a big deal, though
I can read my book

"Hey, Loeb, over here."
A quiet voice, beckoning
"Some brain food for you?"

Yeah, yeah, so funny
"I hear it cures you Z-tards."
"Suck it, you Chupo!"

Fangs curl in a smile
"With pleasure, my undead friend."
I throw down my book

A very loud sigh
I see her in slow motion
Siobhan shakes her head

"Listen, you morons."
She's pointing at me and Carl
"No blood. No sucking."

This makes Maggie laugh
She points at Larry and Matt
"Brainless and Nitwit."

Mags, Siobhan cackle
"A messed up Wizard of Oz."
Which one's Dorothy?

Make a face at them
Try to read my book again
"Who are you kidding?"

Want to ignore him
"I thought Z-tards couldn't read."
He just won't relent

Four Zs in this room
Does Carl have an undead wish?
Siobhan turns around

"You need to cool it."
"What's that, miss high and mighty?
You're the one with this."

"You're making money.
Bottled brains for the Z-tards . . .
Brilliant idea, L."

A sound like thunder
Larry throws his desk at Carl
Nicks a scaly horn

Carl dives like a bat
Larry gives entrails a swing
Lassos the Chupo

Now everyone's up
Even haiku pales to this
I stare at the fight

The door bursts open
A Moses to our freak sea
Fincher pushes through

Anger palpable
She somehow subdues Larry
Carl flits to ceiling

Horn chunk on the floor
Siobhan leans over, grabs it
I raise my eyebrows

Mags has seen her, too
"Whatcha need that for, Siobhan?
More 'cures' for Z-tards?"

Fincher's hand goes up
"I want silence in this room."
We all sit back down

She takes Larry out
But not with a swift kill shot
Just to the VP

She curls her finger
Carl flies crookedly behind
It's so quiet now

Again, we're alone
Matt appears to be sleeping
I pick up my book

I'll show that Chupo
I might slur and enjoy brains
But I'm not stupid

This contest is mine
A zombie apocalypse
At the mic tonight

The Contest

I can't clear my head
Even with all of the holes
Fincher, Siobhan, brains

This is my life, huh?
It's *The Catcher in the Fly*
Lame teen zombie angst

Better write poem
Last minute creative burst
Need to eat a brain

Fresh out of fresh brains
This durian lobe will do
Smells good. Will it work?

Poor brain substitute
Durian is not fresh flesh
Am not inspired

"Pocket durian?
"Boy you are desperate, Loeb!"
Mags laughs her teeth out

My turn's coming up
Chest is fluttering wildly
Not from worms this time

Lifers, Zs, Chupos
All sitting in audience
High school tinderbox

Matt is razzing me
He keeps pointing at Fincher,
who's smiling at me

Swift kick makes him stop
He stumbles into Lifer
My luck is awesome

How original
Popular kid torments geek
Must stifle my yawn

I said that out loud?
Internal monologue fail
Must start shutting mouth

Lifer swears revenge
He's next on stage, though. I'm safe.
It's time to line up

He's a jerk Prufrock
From non-mangled lips, words flow
The crowd goes bonkers

Uh-oh. It's my cue.
I'm trying to find my groove
The world starts spinning

Onstage. Light hurts eyes.
What am I? A vampire now?
Need some new eyelids

Like a bleached femur
Microphone, uninviting
It honks when I speak

Hear heckles from crowd
Durian is stuck in throat
Stammer out my name

"Brains!" I shout at them.
"I'm gonna show you my brains!"
No one gets my joke

Someone throws a shoe
"Get bent retarded zombie!"
I look at Fincher

Imperceptibly
Her lips mouth, "You can do it."
I am energized

Take the microphone
An open mic de-seg night
Surprises them all

"Crashing heads, blood sprays.
They call us barbarians
But they play football."

My simple haiku
There is a beat, then laughing
Some cheering even

"Avoid eye contact
Biggest lesson of this school
Always look away"

There is more laughing
They are laughing with me, though
Not at me for once

"Lifers, Chupos, Zs
Melting pot of dopes and thugs
Or are we just kids?"

Crowd quiets down now
Fincher nods her head for more
Read crumbled paper

"'I Have a Dream' speech
Is it meant for brain eaters?
Meant for goat suckers?"

Stares are quizzical
Even Lifer Prufrock stares
I can't seem to stop

"Why are we afraid?
We have commonality:
Middle school sucks hard!"

"OK, Loeb. Thank you."
Mrs. Fincher drags me off
Crowd is going wild

Enjoy sudden fame
Don't even know if I won
Can't hear over cheers

Somehow she finds me
We're weaving through the tangle
Where are we going?

Projection booth's safe
We have a great view from here
What are we doing?

"Zs aren't so dumb?"
Involuntarily smile
Stupid facial ticks

She doesn't answer
Why did she come and find me?
She touches my face

Hands over my ear
I take it back, embarrassed
She stares, then runs off

Things settling down
This is a weird and good night
Dezombregation

Library

Super dark in here
Couldn't find Maggie or Matt
Need to gather thoughts

Paper in my hand
Sitting alone on the floor
Haiku really works

Lost my mind tonight
Can't let mouth run off like that
But they all loved it

Except for Siobhan
Or maybe she did like it
Lifer enigma

I want to see her
Ask her why she grabbed my hand
What was she doing?

Maybe she likes me
In a like like kind of way
Do I like like her?

Wait. Is it a trick?
Am I her science project?
Gullible Z-tard?

Goo begins to boil
An unpleasant sensation
I have to see her

She should know the truth
Our necrotic hearts break, too
Many black pieces

Siobhan's House

Standing in her yard
Shadows bounce behind windows
Uh-oh, a party

How do I get in?
Ring doorbell; no one answers
Maybe a window?

Arm pokes through the blinds
I'm reenacting E.T.
Without marigolds

Someone shouts. Uh-oh.
Guess I picked the wrong window
Dude's on the toilet

Now he's chasing me
Throw fruit as peace offering
Hits him in the face

This was a mistake
Break all slasher movie rules
And run up the stairs

How did this happen?
Aren't Zs the aggressors?
Not compared to jocks

"Over here, silly."
Hand reaches out, grabs my shirt
What's another rip?

Hiding in back room
Hand lets go of my T-shirt
Of course it's Siobhan

"You looking for me?"
Her eyes are black; she's grinning
I can smell her brains

"How are you tonight?"
She's killing me with small talk
Give her zombie stare

"I thought you liked me."
She's making fun . . . or flirting?
"Sudden change of heart?"

"You mean mine for yours?"
"And he's funny, too, ladies."
"What's your deal, Siobhan?"

"You've been using me.
Zs have feelings, too, you know.
Brain eaters need friends."

She takes a step back.
"Oh, Loeb, you're too serious."
Black curls frame her face

"Just a quick buck, then?
To cure our stupidity,
You sell us snake oil?"

Push open the door
"Loeb. Stop. Please! Loeb! Wait for me!"
Shamble down the stairs

She is after me
"That's not it at all! It's not!"
Try to ignore her

Worse than those movies
Where cute girl makes a dumb bet
To date lonely nerd

"I *do* think you're smart!"
Everyone is staring now
She's making a scene

"Don't talk down to me.
I'm not your charity case.
I'm smart without you."

No one is moving
You could hear a mouse squeaking
Runs from my pant leg

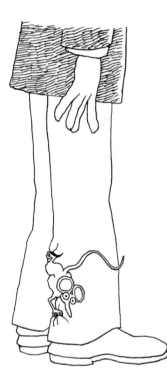

"I made it up, Loeb.
An excuse to get to you.
I think you're too cool."

She's looking at me
Has a funny expression
Head tilted, soft eyes

"Lifer and a Z?
I needed a good reason
to get close to you."

"So you made fake sweat?
To cure my stupidity?
It's so insulting!"

"What else could I do?
To cross invisible line,
to get close to you?"

Time to call her bluff
Corner her with zombie flair
Pin her to the wall

We are face-to-face
She's breathing furiously
I lean in closer

"Don't like your tactics.
Even though I might like you."
Clack my teeth at her

So now who's bluffing?
She turns her head, closes eyes
Her hair smells so good

Pull out my paper
Clear my throat to read poem
She's my microphone

"Siobhan is a girl.
Not a Lifer or a Z,
Just the girl for me."

Worst haiku of all
They're never supposed to rhyme
What am I doing?

"Just the girl for you?
As a friend, or for eating?"
She hazards a smile

"As a friend . . . for now."
Lifers stand in shocked silence
Siobhan kisses me

Walk out together
Did we just make history?
What will Maggie say?

"It's not the sweat, Loeb.
I really do think you're smart.
You're kind of cute, too."

How do I answer?
Don't know if I can trust her
Touch her ivy hair

A Z and an L
Break all the rules together
It's very tempting

"Is my brain safe, Loeb?"
She's relaxing, joshing me
I smile and grab her

Then I take a bite
Juicy part of the left lobe
It's my favorite

She lets out a gasp
It tastes so sweet. Just like brains.
Offer her a bite